W.H. WHEELER

FEARON-PITMAN PUBLISHERS, INC.
Belmont, California

Series Director: Tom Belina
Designer: Richard Kharibian
Cover and illustrations: David Cunningham

ISBN–0–8224–5273–0

Library of Congress Catalog Card Number: 77-82063

Printed in the United States of America.

1. 9 8 7 6 5 4 3 2 1

CONTENTS

CHAPTER 1
DR. GARCIA

Lola Taggert opened her front door. She reached down and pulled the morning paper out from under her cat.

"Morning, Fang. Off my paper," she said.

Fang gave Lola a dirty look and walked into the house.

Lola closed the door. "Let's see what's in the paper today," she said. She sat down to read.

Lola read as many magazines and papers as she could. They gave her ideas for stories. Lola made her living writing and selling stories to magazines.

She sat down at her kitchen table for breakfast. She opened the paper. She read it while she drank a glass of milk.

"Hey, Fang, here is something good," she said. She pointed to a story in the paper. Fang, the cat, was sitting on the chair next to her. Like most cats, he could not have cared less.

"It's about a man named Dr. Thomas Garcia," Lola said. "He is the Director of Asian art at the Harrison Museum. He is going to Borneo."

She looked over at Fang. His eyes were half-closed. He moved his legs a little. Then he closed his eyes the rest of the way and went to sleep.

"Fat lot *you* care, cat," said Lola. "But this is really interesting. The story says that Dr. Garcia is going to Borneo to look for a lost city. A city built high up on the side of a 13,000 foot mountain—Mount Kinabalu. A people called Pumuts once lived there. They were rich and had much gold. But they disappeared years ago. No one knows what happened to the people or to their city—or to their gold. But now Dr. Garcia thinks he may be able to find it."

Lola tore the story out of the paper. She looked at the clock on the wall.

"Almost nine," she said. "Maybe this Dr. Garcia is at the museum by now. I'd sure like to do a story on him and his trip to Borneo."

Lola got up from the table and walked over to the telephone. She picked up the telephone book. She looked up the number of the Harrison Museum.

Dr. Thomas Garcia had just come into his office when the telephone rang.

"Hello?" he said.

"Dr. Garcia?" asked Lola on the other end of the line.

"Yes . . ."

"My name is Lola Taggert. I saw the story about you in the morning paper. I write stories for magazines. I would like to come and talk to you about your trip to Borneo. I think it would make a great story."

"Well, I don't know if *I'm* all that interesting," Dr. Garcia said. "But Borneo sure is. Come on over."

"Great!" said Lola. "How about this morning? Say in an hour or so?"

"Fine," said Dr. Garcia. "See you around 10 or 10:30 then."

The Harrison Museum was not a giant museum. It was housed in an old gray stone building. But it was an important museum. It was one of the top Asian art museums in the country.

Lola drove up the street toward the museum. "Borneo," she said to herself. The word had such a far-away sound.

Lola parked her car near the front of the museum. She went inside. She asked the man at the front desk where to find Dr. Garcia. He pointed to a hall leading from the back of the room. When Lola found Dr. Garcia's office, the door was open. On one wall, she could see all kinds of things from Borneo—blow pipes, head hunting knives, pots, drums, bells, and other things to make music with.

"Dr. Garcia?" called Lola. She walked part way through the open door. "I'm Lola Taggert. May I come in?"

Thomas Garcia wasn't the kind of person you might think would work in a museum. He was in his 30's, tall and strong. Every morning, he ran the two miles from his home to the museum. And then he ran back at night. "If I don't, I'll get fat," he always told people. There might be dust on the old pots in his office, but not on him.

Dr. Garcia turned around at Lola's voice.

"Miss Taggert. Glad you could make it," he said. "Come in and sit down." He pointed to a chair next to his desk. "Tell me what I can do for you."

Lola sat down and took out her note book.

"Well," she said. "We could start with the story about the lost city of the Pumuts—and the gold they were supposed to have."

CHAPTER 2
The Story of the Pumuts

Dr. Garcia sat back in his desk chair.

"The lost city of the Pumuts," he said. "Yes, well, first of all, remember that it's still just a story so far. I believe that there is a lost city on Mount Kinabalu. And I believe that the gold of the Pumuts is there, too. But I might be wrong."

"What do you mean?" asked Lola.

"Well, the story in the paper left out a lot of what I said," Dr. Garcia explained. "The story made it seem that I said there was a lost city for sure. And that there was gold for sure. But I just don't know."

"Then why are you going to Borneo?"

"To find out for sure. You see, in Borneo there are a lot of old stories about Mount Kinabalu. At one time, people believed there was a lake at the top of the mountain. A lake where the Borneo gods lived. Now we know that there is no lake on top. And there may be no lost city, either."

"But you still think there is," Lola said, making some notes in her note book.

"Yes, I do," Dr. Garcia answered. "No one I have ever met has ever seen the city. But almost everyone says that it is there."

"Has anyone ever looked?" Lola asked.

"Oh, yes, many times. But Mount Kinabalu keeps its secrets well. There is jungle all around the mountain. And thick forests on its sides. Heavy rains and thick clouds cover most of the mountain most of the time. If there is a city on the mountain, it will not be easy to find."

"Then what makes you think you can do it?" Lola said, making another note.

"We have some new kinds of equipment," Dr. Garcia said. "New equipment that can find gold from an airplane. In a week we can cover ground that would take years on land. I think we can find the lost city with our new equipment. And the gold—if it is there."

"Mount Kinabalu sounds like a pretty big place," Lola said. "Do you have any idea of just where to start?"

"Yes," Dr. Garcia answered. "If the old stories are true, I know where to look. Somewhere near a place called Low's Gully."

"Low's Gully," said Lola. "That doesn't sound too bad a place."

Dr. Garcia laughed. "You should see it! The sides are walls of rock that go straight up and down for two thousand feet all around! It has never even been climbed into from the north—or from the south, either. There seems to be a way in from the south. But the jungle has stopped everyone who has ever tried."

"But you're going to try," said Lola.

"It's the only way in," Dr. Garcia said. "Yes, I'm going to try—if we pick up signs of the gold from the airplane."

Lola looked at her notes. Then she looked back up at Dr. Garcia. "You keep talking about these old stories," she said. "Just what do these old stories say about the Pumuts?"

"The old stories tell about a people called the Pumuts. They were different from any other people who lived in Borneo—the Dyaks, Ibans, Bajaus, Kayans, and so on. These other peoples were poor. But, say the old stories, the Pumuts were rich. And they had nothing to do with any of these other peoples.

"The stories say that the Pumuts lived all by themselves in a city high on the sides of Mount Kinabalu. They had a gold mine there. They used the gold from their mine to make statues of their gods."

"Their gods?" Lola asked.

"Yes. They believed in many gods. They made a gold statue of each of their gods. They set the statues up in their city on Mount Kinabalu."

Lola had another question. "How does anyone know this really happened?" she asked. "You said that the Pumuts had nothing to do with any other peoples. And that no one seems ever to have visited their city."

Dr. Garcia turned and looked at the knives and blow pipes on his wall. "Right you are," he said. "They didn't want anyone from the outside to ever visit their city. They used knives and blow pipes like those over there to keep people out. Or so the old stories say."

"Then—"

"Let me finish," Dr. Garcia said. "But one day the secret of the gold statues got out. This was a long time ago—more than a hundred years."

"What happened?"

"One day a man—a Pumut—came walking off the mountain. He walked into a small Dusun town many miles from Mount Kinabalu."

"Dusun?" Lola asked.

"Dusun. Another Borneo people. Well, anyway, the man walked into town carrying one of the gold statues. The old stories say he was more dead than alive. He told the people in the town that he was the last of the Pumuts."

Lola was taking notes as fast as she could. "Go on," she said.

"The man begged the Dusun people to let him stay in their town. He said that he was the only Pumut left alive. He said that his people

had done bad things. The gods had become angry. They killed all his people. All but him."

"Why did the gods let him live?" Lola asked.

"To carry out their orders," Dr. Garcia answered. "They told him to take the Pumut's gold statues to a secret place where the water ran hot. He was to throw the statues into the water and leave."

"But you said that he had one of the gold statues with him," Lola said.

"Yes. He threw the other statues into the water. But he kept one. He kept it to remember his people by."

"What happened to the man?" Lola asked. "Did the Dusuns let him stay in their town?"

"Yes. He lived there for many years. Then, when he was an old man, he went back into the jungle. He took the statue with him. He was never seen again. And that was the last of the Pumuts."

"That's some story," Lola said, closing her note book. "Do you really believe it?"

"Enough to go back to Borneo again," Dr. Garcia said. "You see, I was in that Dusun town. There was an old man there who told me the story. He remembered the Pumut man. He was just a boy then, but he remembered the day the Pumut man disappeared into the jungle."

"When are you leaving?" Lola asked.

"I plan to leave in two weeks."

"Can you use some help?"

"What do you mean?"

"I mean I'd like to go along," Lola said. "I'd pay my own way. I'd really like to help you look for those statues."

"I wasn't thinking about the money," Dr. Garcia said. "It's not going to be any Sunday picnic."

"I know that," Lola said. "I know what the jungle is like. My father ran a logging business in South America. I grew up in the jungle. I was 17 when we left."

Dr. Garcia said nothing. He was thinking.

"Come on," Lola said at last. "You won't be sorry. I can take pictures, too."

"That *would* be a help," Dr. Garcia said.

"So?"

Dr. Garcia thought some more. Then he said, "OK, you're on the team. Can you be ready in two weeks?"

"I can be ready in two *hours!*" Lola said.

CHAPTER 3
CAPTAIN UNTUNG

Two weeks later, Dr. Garcia and Lola were on a plane heading across the Pacific Ocean. Their first stop was Honolulu. From there they flew to Tokyo. Then they went on to Hong Kong. They stayed the night to rest from their long trip. Then, the next morning, they got on the plane that would take them across the South China Sea to Borneo.

Lola got her first view of Mount Kinabalu while the plane was still far out over the sea. The great mountain pushed up into the sky like something that still seemed to be growing.

"I can see why they used to think gods lived on the top," Lola said.

"Yes," Dr. Garcia said. "It really is some mountain. There is no other mountain anywhere near as tall in all of Southeast Asia."

Then they felt the plane start to come down. "We are getting ready to land," Dr. Garcia said.

They flew over a few small islands. Then the plane was over the land. Lola looked down. She could see a river cutting its way through the green jungle. And she could see some white buildings by the sea. It was the town of Kota Kinabalu, the main Borneo city.

The plane turned and started down for the airport. They touched down a few minutes later. The plane pulled up to a stop near the airport building. To Lola's surprise, it looked much like any other airport. Somehow, she thought the airport would be made out of sticks and grass. That was her idea of how a Borneo airport should look, anyway.

Men from the airport pushed stairs on wheels up to the plane. Then Lola and Dr. Garcia got up from their seats. They walked behind the other people on the plane to the plane door.

Lola stepped out onto the stairs. The hot air hit her like wet fire. Dr. Garcia could see the look on her face. "Yes, it's hot in Borneo," he said. "But you will get used to it."

"I hope so," Lola answered.

They started down the stairs and then walked into the airport building.

"They will check our papers over there," Dr. Garcia said. He pointed to a group of people on the other side of the room.

As they stood in line, Lola looked around her. There were people of many different races and colors in the room—Chinese, Malays, Filipinos, Indians, Europeans, Japanese, as well as Dusuns and Dyaks. Dr. Garcia had told her that Borneo was a land of many different peoples. Now Lola could see that it was true.

Then it was Lola's turn to have her papers checked. The man at the desk looked them over and stamped them. Then he turned to Dr. Garcia. "May I have your papers, please?"

Dr. Garcia handed the man his papers.

"Ah, Dr. Thomas Garcia," the man said. "There is someone here to meet you." He stamped Dr. Garcia's papers and handed them back. He waved to a man standing by the door. The man walked over.

"Dr. Garcia?" the man said. Lola could see that he was an army captain.

"Yes," Dr. Garcia said. The two men shook hands.

"I'm Captain Mat Salleh Untung."

"Pleased to meet you," said Dr. Garcia. "It is nice of you to come and meet us here."

"When the Chief Minister got your letter," said Captain Untung, "he called our office. They asked me to help you during your visit."

"Thank you," Dr. Garcia said. "We can use all the help we can get. I'd like you to meet Lola Taggert. She will be working with me."

Captain Untung looked surprised. Lola could tell what he was thinking. "Don't worry, Captain," she said. "I am very used to jungle trips. I grew up in a jungle."

"Oh, I'm sure . . ." Captain Untung said. "It's just that . . . the Borneo jungle is the most dangerous in the world. There are many kinds of wild animals. Perhaps it would be better if you stayed in town . . ."

"My dear Captain Untung," Lola said. "I am not afraid of wild animals. Sometime I'll tell you about how I killed a bear with just my hands. It jumped out of a tree at me. That was in a jungle in South America."

Captain Untung's mouth fell open. "A *bear?*"

"A bear," said Lola.

Captain Untung looked at Lola and then at Dr. Garcia. Dr. Garcia was smiling. The army captain didn't know what to say. At last, he turned and said, "I'll go pick up your bags. Then I'll drive you into town."

While they were waiting for Captain Untung to get back, Dr. Garcia said, "A bear? You will have to tell *me* about that bear some time. I never heard of any bears in the jungles of South America. And I never heard of any bears *any-where* jumping out of trees."

Lola laughed. "There never was any bear. I made the whole thing up. Captain Untung has some rather old ways of thinking about women.

I thought it best to put him straight right from the start."

Dr. Garcia laughed, too. "Well, you sure did that. But remember, this isn't back home."

"Don't worry," Lola said. "I'll be good!"

A few minutes later Captain Untung came back. "I had your bags and equipment checked through," he said. "They are in my car. I'll drive you to your hotel. Where are you staying?"

"At the Api Hotel," Dr. Garcia said.

"The Api?" Captain Untung said. "You know that the Api is kind of out-of-the-way. I thought you might be staying at the Trusan or the Kwan Chai Hotel. They are both new. And right in town."

"We are staying at the Api Hotel because it *is* out-of-the-way," Dr. Garcia said. "The less people know about why we are here, the better. We don't want any company on our hunt for the gold."

"I understand," Captain Untung said. "We will see to it that there is no trouble."

The got into Captain Untung's army Land Rover and drove into town.

CHAPTER 4
THE CHINESE STATUE

As they drove into town, Captain Untung and Dr. Garcia talked. But Lola wasn't listening. She was too busy looking at the sights along the way.

Then they drove into Kota Kinabalu. Again, as at the airport, Lola was surprised. Most of the buildings were new. And very clean. The people in the streets—Chinese, Malays, and Dusuns—were dressed much like anyone anywhere else. Somehow, she thought they would dress in a different way in Borneo.

At last, they got to the Api Hotel. It was on the far side of town.

Captain Untung helped them check into their rooms.

"Will you meet us later for dinner, Captain?" Dr. Garcia asked.

"I'd be happy to," Captain Untung answered. "Perhaps Miss Taggert will tell me more about that bear over dinner."

Lola smiled. "I'll tell you about the pack of wild pigs that I beat off, too."

Dr. Garcia couldn't help laughing.

Captain Untung only smiled.

Captain Untung came back to the hotel at six. The sun was going down, but it was still very hot. They decided to stay in the hotel and eat. A young Chinese boy in a white coat showed them to their table.

There were not many people in the place. Two men were drinking at the table next to them. There were a few other people at other tables.

Captain Untung held up his glass in front of him. "To the hunt, my friends," he said.

Lola and Dr. Garcia both lifted their glasses. "To the hunt," they both said.

"Going hunting, Mat?" a voice said. A young man had come up behind Captain Untung's chair. Captain Untung turned.

"Pete!" he said to the young man. "I thought you were in Labuan."

"I just got back this morning."

Captain Untung turned back to Lola and Dr. Garcia. "This is my good friend Pete Summers," he said. "Pete is an American like you."

"Glad to meet you," Lola said.

"Hello," Dr. Garcia said.

"I didn't mean to break into your dinner," Pete Summers said. "I just wanted to say hello to my friend Captain Untung. I haven't seen him in three months."

"Any friend of Captain Untung is a friend of ours," Dr. Garcia said. "Won't you join us?"

"Yes, please do," Lola said.

Pete pulled up a chair and sat down. "Mind if I ask what you're hunting?" he asked.

Captain Untung looked at Dr. Garcia. "It's OK," he said. "Pete knows how to keep a secret. I have known him for five years."

Dr. Garcia looked at Pete. "Don't tell anyone," he said. "But we are here to hunt for the statues of the Pumuts."

"Not those gold ones, I hope," Pete said.

"So you know the story," Lola said.

"Sure," Pete answered. "I think everyone in Borneo knows that story. That was one of the first things I heard about when I first moved here. And that was a while back."

"How long have you lived here?" Lola asked.

"Since I was 14. My father was in the logging business on Labuan. That's an island about 90 miles from here. He was killed in an accident a few years ago. I thought about going back. But by then Borneo had become my real home. So I just stayed on."

"My father was in the logging business, too," Lola said.

"Small world," Pete said with a smile.

"Pete is a real old Borneo hand," Captain Untung said. "He can speak Malay, Dusun, Dyak, and–"

"—English," Pete laughed. "But tell me more about the gold statues, Dr. Garcia. You're not really going to go looking for them, are you?"

"Yes, we are," Dr. Garcia answered.

"But that's just an old story about those statues," Pete said. "They aren't real. I even looked for them myself. I've been all over Mount Kinabalu looking for them. That was before I got smart and gave up. There is nothing on that mountain. Not on any part of it."

"Not even in Low's Gully?" Dr. Garcia asked.

"Low's Gully!" Pete said. Then he laughed. "You can't get into Low's Gully. No one can. There is no way."

"Then we may have to find a way," Dr. Garcia said with a smile. "If I'm right about that picture I saw."

"What do you mean?" Pete asked.

"Yes," said Captain Untung. "What picture you saw?"

"I'll have to back up a bit first," Dr. Garcia said. He told them about the man in the Dusun town near Mount Kinabalu. How the man said he remembered the Pumut man with the statue. How the Pumut man disappeared into the jungle one day, taking the statue with him. Then he told them about the picture.

"I had just returned to the United States from my last trip to Borneo," Dr. Garcia said. "I didn't really believe the old man in the Dusun town. I thought that maybe he had made up the story just to please me."

"Happens all the time," Pete said. "People tell you what they think you want to hear."

"Yes," Dr. Garcia said. "But then a friend sent me a picture. It was a picture of a statue in a museum in China. But it didn't look like a Chinese statue. It looked like it was made in Borneo. And it was gold."

"You don't mean—" Captain Untung said.

"Yes," Dr. Garcia answered. "I think it was a picture of one of the Pumut statues."

"But how did it get to China?" Pete asked.

"That's what I wanted to know," Dr. Garcia said. "So I wrote to the museum. They said they got it from the son of a man who once lived in Borneo. The man was a Chinese trader. He had a store on the Kinabatangan River. And that river is not far from the Dusun town I told you about."

"And where is the statue now?" Pete asked.

"No one knows," Dr. Garcia said. "It disappeared in World War II. The Chinese museum only has a picture of it now."

Pete said. "Well, maybe those statues *are* real, after all."

"I think they might be," Dr. Garcia said. "If there was one statue, there may be others."

"But how did the Chinese trader get the statue in the first place?" Captain Untung asked Dr. Garcia.

"I think someone found it in the jungle," Dr. Garcia said. "I think the old Pumut man went off into the jungle to die. He took the statue with him. It stayed there for many years. Then someone just found it—probably while out hunting. Then whoever found it traded it to the Chinese trader for store goods. And the trader's son took it back with him when he went back to live in China."

Just then, Pete looked at his watch. "Hey, I've got to go," he said. "I'm supposed to meet a man about some business I have on Labuan."

"Aren't you going to stay and have dinner with us?" Lola asked.

"I'd love to," Pete answered. "But I can't. How about tomorrow? I'd like to hear more about your hunt for the statues."

"We will be at the airport most of tomorrow," Dr. Garcia said. "We have to get our equipment put on the plane we will use."

"Well," said Pete. "How about if I meet you at the airport for lunch then?"

"Fine," Dr. Garcia answered. "See you then."

Pete got up and left. The others stayed and ordered dinner. They talked more about the statues. When they finished eating, they got up and left. The two men at the next table watched them go.

Sam Townsend and Carl Fitzer had just come to Kota Kinabalu. They had been down in Brunei, hanging around the oil fields. Fitzer was a big man. He was in his 50's, but he was very strong. He had almost no hair. His few friends called him "Hog." Townsend was about 45. He was tall and thin. He had a long cut on one side of his face.

"What do you think, Hog?" asked Townsend. "You hear what they said?"

"Enough to get me interested," Fitzer answered. "What I think is that we got us some easy money. Big money."

"Very easy money," said Townsend. "They find it. We take it."

"And," said Fitzer, "we don't leave them around to talk about it."

CHAPTER **5**

Over the Mountain

When Pete got to the airport the next day, there was no sign of Dr. Garcia and the others. He looked all around. Then he saw an army plane at the far end of the airport. It was painted green. There were three people next to it working on it.

Pete walked over to where the plane was. He saw Captain Untung working on the plane. "What are you doing way over here?" Pete asked his friend.

Captain Untung looked up. "Oh, hello, Pete. So you found us."

"Only after a lot of looking."

Dr. Garcia stepped out of the plane. "We didn't want a lot of people watching what we were doing," he said.

"What are you doing?" Pete asked.

"Getting this plane ready to hunt for the statues," Dr. Garcia answered. "Captain Untung will fly it. We are putting two kinds of special equipment on board. One kind will spot any place on the ground that gives off a lot of heat. The other kind can spot gold."

"And what happens if you find something?" Pete asked. "You can't land a plane on Mount Kinabalu."

"If we find something," said Lola, "we come back on foot."

"When will the plane be ready?" Pete asked.

"It's almost ready now," Captain Untung answered. "We will take it up tomorrow morning as soon as the sun comes up. Before the mountain gets covered up with clouds."

"Want to come along?" Dr. Garcia asked. "There's room in the plane."

"Hey, thanks a lot," Pete said. "I'd like that. Now let me buy you all some lunch."

"Sounds good," Captain Untung said. They started to walk back to the airport building. They did not see the two men watching them from across the landing field.

Townsend and Fitzer had been watching them since they got to the airport. "Looks like they are going to use a plane to hunt for the statues," Fitzer said. "So how are we going to follow them?"

"We can't," Townsend said. "But if they find anything, they will have to go in on foot. Then maybe we can follow them. Right now, we just keep an eye on them."

"I think we have seen enough for now," Fitzer said. "Let's get out of here before someone spots us."

Early the next morning, Captain Untung picked up Lola and Dr. Garcia at their hotel. They drove to the airport. Pete was already there, waiting for them.

Captain Untung gassed up the plane and checked the controls. Dr. Garcia checked the special equipment.

Then they were off, heading for Mount Kinabalu. They could see it ahead of them, pushing out of the jungle like a sleeping giant.

Lola looked down at the jungle below them. It was solid and thick.

"If we find anything," Pete said, "we will have to come back through *that.*" He pointed at the green jungle.

"*We* will have to come back . . . ?" Lola said.

Pete smiled. "Yes, *we,*" he said. "I'd like to come with you. I know the mountain better than any of you. I could be of real help. How about it?"

Dr. Garcia turned in his seat. "I thought you said you didn't believe there were any statues."

Pete laughed. "I changed my mind. Now, can I come with you?"

"OK," said Dr. Garcia. "Sounds like we would have a hard time keeping you from coming if we tried. So, yes, you can come."

"Great!" said Pete.

With each passing minute Mount Kinabalu seemed a bit bigger. They were getting close now. Lola could see the thick forests on the side of the mountain. She could also see where the trees stopped growing. That was where it got too high for trees to grow. Then there was nothing but sharp rocks pushing up into the deep blue sky. It was still early in the day, but already the clouds were beginning to form over the mountain.

As they got close to the mountain, winds began to knock the plane about. Captain Untung had to fight to keep control. "I won't be able to fly over the top," he told the others. "This is about as close as I can come."

"Can you take us over Low's Gully?" Dr. Garcia asked.

"I'll try. I'll come at it from the south."

A few minutes later, they were over the south side of the giant mountain. Clouds were starting to form now, and parts of the mountain were already covered.

"See anything?" Lola asked Pete.

"No. How about you?"

Lola looked out the window on the other side of the plane. "Nothing yet. Just rocks and clouds," she answered.

Captain Untung began flying in a circle. "It's somewhere around here," he told the others. "Keep a sharp eye."

The wind was pushing the plane around in the sky like a toy. They all had to hold on tight, even with their seat belts on.

Then Dr. Garcia said, "Look! There it is. Low's Gully."

Off to the right, they could see it. Low's Gully looked like a giant hole on the side of the mountain. Its dark gray walls dropped straight down. The bottom was covered with thick white clouds.

"I'll get the heat finding equipment ready," Dr. Garcia said.

Lola handed him a box. Dr. Garcia opened it and took out a small gray box with controls on the top. Then he took out a short black pipe. It had glass on one end. From the other end ran a blue and yellow wire.

He hooked up the wire to the gray box. Then he reached down to the floor of the plane. He took a cover off a hole that had been cut in the

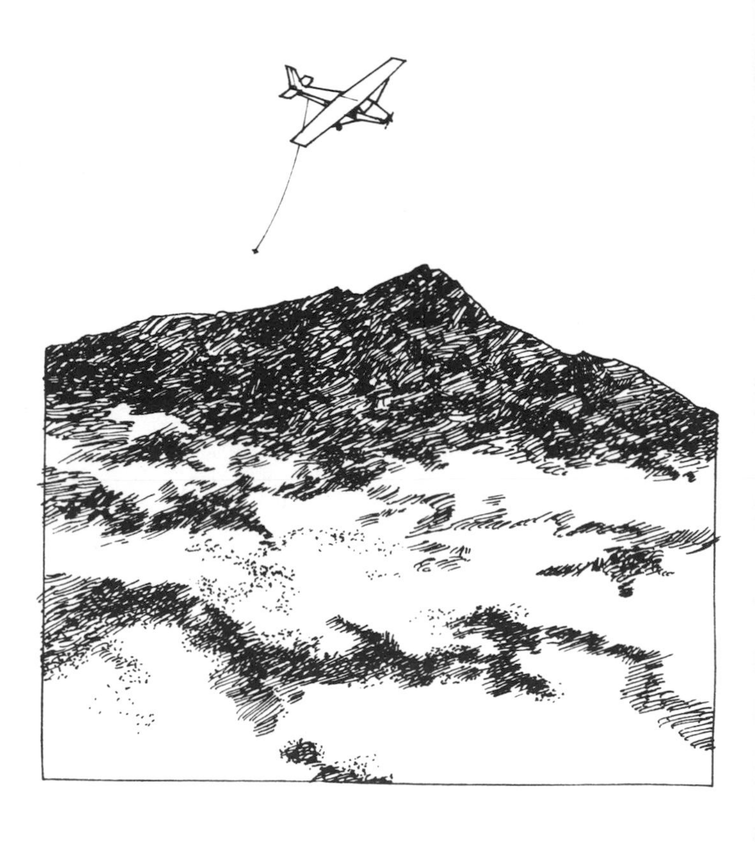

floor. He slowly let the black pipe out through the hole, feeding out wire a bit at a time.

"All set," he said, turning on the controls on the gray box.

Captain Untung turned the plane around and made another pass over Low's Gully.

"Anything?" Pete asked Dr. Garcia.

Dr. Garcia was looking at a light on the gray box. It was not on. "No, nothing yet," he said. "Maybe we are too high. Captain Untung, can you come down a little?"

"Not much," Captain Untung answered. "Not in this wind. But I'll try." The plane was rocking up and down in the wind.

They flew in large circles, flying over Low's Gully again and again.

"If we don't find anything soon, I'll have to head back," Captain Untung said.

Just then, the light on the gray box started flashing.

"I've got something!" Dr. Garcia said. "The light shows that there is something hot down there. Lola, give me the gold-finding equipment. Quick!"

Lola handed Dr. Garcia another pipe. It looked like the first one, but was covered with small round holes. Dr. Garcia pulled up the first pipe. He started to let the gold-finding pipe down on another wire. Then, suddenly, the wind pushed the plane up very fast. Dr. Garcia grabbed for the wire. But it was too late. They watched the special equipment fall into Low's Gully, far below.

No one said anything for a minute. Then Pete turned in his seat and said, "Did you bring another one with you?"

"No," Dr. Garcia answered. "Each one costs $10,000."

"Oh. Well, now what?"

Dr. Garcia tapped Captain Untung on the back. "Let's head back."

CHAPTER **6**

PLANS ARE MADE

It was early afternoon when they landed at the Kota Kinabalu airport. Captain Untung brought the plane in and stopped. Fitzer and Townsend were standing by a window in the airport building.

"There they are," said Fitzer. "They are getting out of the plane."

"Do you think they found anything?" Townsend asked.

"Maybe," said Fitzer. "They are doing a lot of talking. They could be talking about what they found."

"But they don't look too happy," Townsend said. "If they found something, they would be laughing and smiling, wouldn't they?"

"Maybe, maybe not," said Fitzer. "Let's try to find out. They have to come through this door. Better they don't see us together too

much. You go over to the door by the street. I'll stay here. I'll try to hear what they are saying as they come in. Then you follow them out the other door and do the same."

"Right," said Fitzer. He walked away.

Pete opened the door for the other three. "Well, we found the hot spot, if nothing else," he was saying to Dr. Garcia.

"*A* hot spot, Pete," Dr. Garcia answered. "There could be many."

"Well, I say it's worth a trip up the river to see," Pete went on.

They walked past Townsend without taking note of him.

But Lola wondered what he was doing standing by the door. "Uh, Pete," she said. "Let's talk about this later, OK?"

They kept on walking through the airport building.

"Did you see that man by the door?" Lola asked in a low voice.

"What man?" Pete asked.

"Don't turn around," said Captain Untung. "He is over by the door we just came through."

"So you saw him, too," Lola said.

"Yes," said Captain Untung.

"Do you know him?" Lola asked.

"No. But I think he was sitting near us last night at the hotel."

"Do you think he heard what we were saying?" Pete asked.

"I don't know," Captain Untung said. "But from now on, let's be careful about what we say when there are others around."

They walked through the door to the street, not seeing Fitzer. He followed them out and watched them as they got into Captain Untung's car and drove away.

"Did you get anything?" asked Townsend, walking up behind Fitzer.

"No," said Fitzer. "They may be on to us. No one said a word when they came past me. Did you catch anything?"

"Enough, I think," said Townsend. "They found *something* on the mountain, that's for sure. One of them was talking about a 'hot spot.' And about taking a trip up the river to find it."

"Nothing said about the gold statues?" Fitzer asked.

"No, just about a hot spot."

"I wonder what that could be," Fitzer said.

"I don't know," Townsend said. "But I think we are going to find out. We will keep a close watch on them. If they move, we move. We had better get ready to go up river if we have to."

Captain Untung stopped his car in front of the hotel. The four of them went inside. They found a place to sit where they were alone. They could see anyone who came near. No one could hear what they were saying.

"Remember the man who walked out of the airport behind us?" Lola said. "I think we have seen him before, too. He was sitting with the other man at the table next to us last night."

"But even if they *did* hear us," said Dr. Garcia, "what can they do?"

"Here, nothing," Captain Untung said. "But in the jungle, it is a different matter."

"I don't think there is much reason to worry about those two," Pete said. "Remember, they have no idea where we are going."

"That's true," Captain Untung said. "So let's get on with planning the trip up river. It will take three or four days to get ready. We will have to get all of our food and equipment together. And plan on getting the boats we will need. If you still want to go, that is."

Dr. Garcia looked at him. "It may be a waste of time and money," he said to Captain Untung. "We have already lost the $10,000 gold-finding equipment. I just don't know. . . ."

"If we don't go," Lola said, "you will never know. I mean, never know if the hot spot we found is the place where the statues are."

"Lola is right," Captain Untung said.

Dr. Garcia didn't say anything for a minute. He was thinking. At last, he said, "All right. We will go."

The other three broke out in big smiles.

"Let's start planning," Pete said.

"There is only one way to get anywhere near Low's Gully," Captain Untung said. "We will have to go up the river from Sandakan."

"Sandakan?" Lola said. "Where is that?"

"On the other side of the state," said Pete. "About 150 miles from here."

"We can fly there in the plane," Captain Untung said. "Sandakan is at the mouth of the Kinabatangan River. That is the river that goes up toward Mount Kinabalu."

Dr. Garcia took a map from his pocket. He showed it to Lola. "Here's Sandakan," he said, pointing to the map. "And here's the river."

"But we will need to change boats two or three times," Pete said.

"Why is that?" Lola asked.

"Near Sandakan, the river is wide," Pete explained. "But as you go up the river, it gets less and less wide. We will have to change boats at a place called Kuamut. It is just a small Dusun town in the jungle. We will get a smaller boat in Kuamut. We will leave the other boat there until we get back."

"And we will have to change again," Captain Untung said. "When we get to a place called Tampasak. There the river becomes small. There are many rocks in the water, too. We will need to use dug-out canoes to get up the river after Tampasak."

"And finally," said Pete, "we will have to walk when we get to the head of the river. We will have to go through the jungle and up the south side of Mount Kinabalu. Then we will try to get into Low's Gully."

"And look for the hot spot—and the statues," said Dr. Garcia.

Lola was looking at the map. "It looks hard even on paper," she said.

"It will be," Captain Untung said. "Are you still sure you want to go?"

"Please, Captain," she said. "Don't start that again. I'm running out of wild animal stories."

Captain Untung did not understand.

In a bar across town, Townsend and Fitzer were also looking at a map.

"They said they were going up river," Townsend said. "The question is, which river? There are lots of rivers."

"But not many that go near Mount Kinabalu. It's got to be one of these three," Fitzer said.

Townsend finished his drink and ordered another. "But which one?" he said.

CHAPTER 7
THE KINABATANGAN

The next day, Dr. Garcia started buying the food and equipment they would need. Pete and Lola went with him. They bought dry food—food that would not go bad in the hot, wet jungle. They also bought long knives to cut their way through the jungle.

Townsend and Fitzer were also buying food and equipment. But they were careful not to let themselves be seen by Dr. Garcia or the others. They did not want them to know that they were going to follow them.

Two days later, Townsend and Fitzer had everything they needed. But they still didn't know which river Dr. Garcia was going up.

They were sitting in a run-down bar next to the fish market. The smell of fish was strong in the hot morning air. Large black flies were all over the table they were sitting at.

Townsend was studying the map again. "It's got to be one of these three rivers, Hog," he said to Fitzer.

"I know that," Fitzer answered. "But we still don't know which one. One river goes toward Mount Kinabalu from the north. One goes toward the mountain from the south. And the third one goes to it from the east. It could be any of them."

"Wait a minute!" Townsend said, pointing at the map. "I've got it!"

"You know which river?" Fitzer asked.

"No, not yet. But we *will* know. As soon as we find out how they plan to get to the mouth of the river."

"I don't understand."

"It's simple," Townsend said. "Just look at the map. If they take their plane, then it's the Kinabatangan River. There is no place to land at the other two rivers."

"What if they don't take the plane?"

"The river to the north can be reached by Land Rover. But the only way to reach the mouth of the river to the east is by sea. They would have to take a boat from Kota Kinabalu to get there."

"Hey," said Fitzer. "I get it! So all we have to do is watch them when they leave. Watch to see if they leave by plane, car, or boat."

"Right! So let's get watching," Townsend said. They paid for their drinks and left.

They walked to a small eating place across the street from the Api Hotel. They could see anyone coming to or going from the hotel. But they could not be seen from the outside.

The next morning, Townsend and Fitzer watched Captain Untung drive up to the hotel. Pete was with him. They saw Lola and Dr. Garcia get into the car.

"They are heading for the airport," Fitzer said to his friend.

"So it's the Kinabatangan River," Townsend said. "Come on! Let's get our equipment. Then we will buy tickets to fly to Sandakan. They won't even know they are being followed."

It was just before noon when the plane got to Sandakan. Captain Untung flew over Sandakan Bay and landed at the airport outside of town. An army Land Rover was waiting for them. The driver loaded all their food and equipment into the car. Then he drove them to a place near the mouth of the Kinabatangan River, a few miles away.

Pete knew a man there who rented boats. They rented a large white boat. It was an old boat, but the engine ran well. They loaded everything on board and started up the river.

The Kinabatangan River was wide here. Thick green jungle grew right down to the river banks on both sides. But here and there, the jungle had been cut away. Lola could see gardens and small farms in these places. There were also some houses. Like most houses in Borneo, they were up on posts. They had metal roofs. The wood walls were not painted and there was no glass in the windows.

They also passed a few logging camps. Lola could see many giant logs floating in the river. She knew that they would float them down to Sandakan to be cut into boards.

All afternoon they headed up the river. There were few houses or farms now. And the river was not as wide as before. Lola could hear birds calling out from the jungle on both sides. Every now and then, she caught sight of one flying. When she did, she took a picture of it. She also took pictures of other things along the river.

About five in the afternoon, they came to a small town on the banks of the river. It was just a few houses, a small school, and one store—a store that sold everything.

"This is the town of Lamag," Captain Untung said. "We will stay here for the night. The sun will soon be going down. We cannot run the boat at night."

About 30 miles behind them, Fitzer and Townsend also stopped for the night.

The next morning, bright and early, they set out again. Pete was steering the boat. They could not go as fast as they had the day before. The river was not so deep or so wide.

It took them all day to reach the next town—Kuamut. This town also had a small store. Captain Untung walked up the steps to the store. He talked with the man who owned the store. He told him that they needed to rent a small boat. They needed a boat that could go where their large boat could not.

Lola wondered if it would be hard to rent a boat. But Pete explained that everyone who lived along the river had a boat. So renting boats was not a problem.

Kuamut also had a small school for the children who lived there. And that was where they stayed that night. In the morning, after a breakfast of cold meat, they set out in a small boat. They would leave the large boat until they got back.

The small boat had a home-made grass roof over it to keep out the burning sun. But it was still very hot. And now that the river was not so wide, there were flies. The air was thick with them. And they loved to bite.

They went up the river for two more days in the small boat. Now there was nothing but jungle on both sides of the river. Tall trees pushed up into the sky. They could see monkeys in some of the trees watching as the boat passed. They also saw packs of wild pigs that came down to the river to drink.

"Are those the kind you beat off with a stick?" Captain Untung asked Lola.

"Yes," she lied. "But in South American jungles the wild pigs are much bigger."

At last, they came to the last place on the river where people lived. This was a place called Tampasak. It was not really a town. The people there all lived in one long building up on posts called a longhouse. They had a few small gardens. They also hunted with blow pipes and fished in the river. They wore very few clothes.

The people spoke a different kind of Dusun. Captain Untung could not understand them. But Pete could. Pete asked the Head Man at the longhouse to rent them some dug-out canoes. The man said he would be glad to.

The people were very happy to see people from the outside. The Head Man asked them to stay the night in their longhouse. Pete said that they would be happy to stay with them.

That evening, they ate the last fresh food they would have for a while—wild pig and fresh fish. The people in the longhouse played music and danced for them.

In the morning, they said good-bye and put their equipment in two dug-out canoes. The river was not deep here. And there were many rocks in it. It was hard going. By the time the sun was going down, they had only gone about seven miles.

And as the sun was setting that day, the people of Tampasak had yet two more people from the outside world—Fitzer and Townsend.

CHAPTER 8
The Jungle

It took them another three days to reach the head waters of the river. By now they were all very tired. At times, they had to get out of the dug-out canoes and pull them past rocks in the river. Their feet and legs were cut from sharp stones in the river. And their hands were red and hurting from paddling all day.

But the worst was yet to come. Ahead of them was giant Mount Kinabalu—and Low's Gully.

They pulled the dug-out canoes up on the banks of the river. It was no more than a small stream now.

Pete looked into the green jungle ahead of them. "Low's Gully is that way," he said.

"How long will it take us to get there?" Lola asked, putting on her back pack.

"A week, maybe more," Pete answered. "But getting *into* Low's Gully itself may take another week—if we *can* get in."

Dr. Garcia checked his map. Then he said, "Well, let's get started."

Captain Untung picked up his gun and moved forward. "Watch out for snakes," he said to the others. "We have more snakes in Borneo than anywhere else in the world."

But snakes were not the problem. The problem was leeches. The jungle was filled with them. They looked like little black worms. They hung on the bottoms of leaves. When they felt some animal coming, they dropped onto it. When they filled up on the animal's blood, they dropped to the ground.

The leeches liked people's blood, too. And you couldn't even feel them doing it. Lola and the others soon had leech bites all over their arms and legs. And the leeches wouldn't even leave them alone when they were sleeping. Every morning all four of them woke up with fresh blood on their arms and legs from leech bites. There were leech bites even on their faces.

The jungle was so thick that they could not see the sun. Even at noon the green light shining down through the trees was not very bright. Much of the time they had to cut their way through the thick forest with their knives. They didn't know it, but they were leaving a very easy trail to follow.

Through the jungle they went. Up and down hills. Across small streams. The streams made many turns through the hills. Because of this, sometimes they had to cross the same stream four or five times in an hour.

When they weren't wet from crossing streams, they were wet from the rain. It rained three or four times a day. The clouds would just open up. It would rain cats and dogs for an hour, then stop. Two hours later, it would rain again just as hard.

"Now I know why they sometimes call a jungle a 'rain forest,'" Lola said after it had rained yet again that day.

"Well, look at it this way," Pete said. "We never have to worry about not having enough drinking water."

Lola tried to smile. But it was too much work. Her hair was in her eyes. Her clothes were wet through. There were leech bites on her arms and legs and cuts from sharp jungle plants. And she had lost a lot of weight from all the hard work.

The other three didn't look any better. They had decided to rest until the rain stopped. Now it had stopped. But not one of them felt much like getting back up. The jungle air was very still and hot. The rain had not cooled things off one bit.

At last, Dr. Garcia got to his feet. "Come on," he said. "I'll lead the way." He started walking.

Pete said, "You're going the wrong way."

Dr. Garcia stopped. He also found it too much work to smile. "Sorry about that," he said at last. "Just a little tired, I guess."

They got up and moved forward.

The land began to go up now. They were nearing Mount Kinabalu. Soon the jungle began to change. There were different kinds of trees and plants. It was still jungle, but it was not so hot now.

"Look!" said Dr. Garcia, as they walked along. Next to a dead tree was a flower. It was red and black and orange. And it was three feet across.

"That's a *Rafflesia,*" Pete said. "The biggest flower in the world. It grows only on Mount Kinabalu."

Lola went over to smell it. She made a face. "It smells like spoiled meat," she said. She took a picture of it. Then they moved on.

The land was getting high now. They were on the side of the mountain. But the jungle was as thick as ever. Some of the giant trees were more than one hundred feet high.

They climbed all the next day, stopping only to rest and eat. They knew that if they made too many stops to rest, they would lose the will to go on.

Finally, around noon of the 10th day, they spotted Low's Gully. Its rock walls went straight up into the sky above.

"No one has ever got this close from the south before," Pete said.

"Maybe," Dr. Garcia said. "But don't forget the Pumuts. They may have built their city here. If the old stories are true."

They looked for a way in for the next four days, without luck. They were all very tired by now. And their food was beginning to run low. No one said anything about it, but all of them were thinking about giving up and going back.

That was just before they found the old path.

CHAPTER 9
Pool of the Gods

Someone had cut the path into Low's Gully a long time ago. The old path was covered over with trees and plants. But it was a way in. Dr. Garcia led the way in, cutting away the trees and plants with his knife.

It was very hard work. It took two days. But at last, the four of them stood on the bottom of Low's Gully. The rock walls went straight up on three sides. They were so high they just disappeared into the clouds above.

And there in front of them was the lost city of the Pumuts. Lola thought there would be more than what there was. Only a few stone walls of some of the buildings were still standing. There was nothing left of the rest of the city.

Behind the city were great piles of rocks.

"The hot spot must be up there," Pete said.

"Well, what are we waiting for?" Lola said.

They set off over the rocks. Two hours later they had still not found anything. They stopped to rest by a little stream. Lola took a cup out of her pack. She reached down into the water to fill her cup. "Hey!" she said, pulling her hand back fast. "This water is *hot!*"

"You're right," Dr. Garcia said. "We must be very near the hot spot."

They all got up and started as fast as they could along the stream. Soon they came to a pool of water. It was about 15 feet across. The water was very dark and very hot.

"It's a hot spring!" Captain Untung said.

Dr. Garcia was taking something out of his pack. It was a special diving suit. With it, a person could dive into very hot water without being cooked alive.

"I hope this diving suit works," Dr. Garcia said, getting ready to step into the water. "That water is really hot–it's wet fire."

"Good luck," said Lola, taking a picture.

In a few seconds he was under the water. They could not see him in the dark water. A minute passed.

"Do you think he is all right?" Pete asked. "He has been down a long time."

But just then Dr. Garcia's arm shot up out of the water. In his hand was a gold statue!

Everyone gave a happy shout.

Dr. Garcia made several more dives. Each time he brought up another gold statue. Finally, about an hour later, he came up empty-handed. He climbed out of the pool. "That's it," he said. "There are no more down there."

They all stood looking down at the gold statues. The last ones brought up were still too hot to touch without diving gloves.

"They really are something," Pete said.

"They sure are," said a strange voice.

It was Fitzer. He was holding a gun. Next to him was Townsend. He had a gun, too.

"Where did you come from?" Lola said.

"We followed you," said Fitzer. "It was easy. You did most of the work for us."

"What do you want?" Dr. Garcia said.

"The gold," said Townsend. "What else?"

Fitzer moved in front of Dr. Garcia, next to the pool. Townsend stood a few feet away. He kept his gun pointed at the others. Fitzer waved at Dr. Garcia with his gun. He pointed to one of the statues with his other hand. "We will start with *that* one," he said. "Hand it over."

Dr. Garcia picked up the statue with his gloves. "Sure," he said. "If that's what you

want." He threw the statue at Fitzer's gun hand. It took Fitzer by surprise. He tried to catch it with his other hand.

He screamed as the hot statue touched his hand. He jumped back. His gun went off with a loud bang. He lost his footing and fell into the hot pool. He screamed again and then sank from sight. The statue went down with him.

Townsend had reached out to try to help Fitzer. It was the chance Captain Untung needed. He grabbed his gun and pointed it at Townsend. "Drop the gun!" he shouted.

Townsend could see that there was nothing he could do for his friend. He let the gun slip from his hand.

No one said anything for a second. Dr. Garcia was looking down into the dark pool of hot water. He was holding his arm.

"Did he hit you?" Lola asked.

"Just missed," Dr. Garcia said. "He tore a hole in my diving suit."

Captain Untung asked Pete to get some rope from his pack to tie Townsend up. As Pete was getting the rope, Captain Untung said to Townsend, "Well, your friend got his wish. He got the gold he wanted."

"Can't you do anything?" Townsend said to Dr. Garcia.

"Sorry. There is a hole in my diving suit. I can't go down again. Even if it would do any good."

"What about the gold statue?" Pete asked.

"We will leave that down there, too. Maybe it is best that way."

"Yes," said Captain Untung. "We have enough statues for our museum here in Borneo. And for your museum, too. Perhaps it is best to leave one statue to watch over this place."

In the sky above, the clouds parted for just a second. A flash of sun made the waters bright.